...en King studied in Bath and lives in London. ...use *Noses on Toast*, his first book for children, ...n the Gold Nestlé Children's Prize. He is the ...thor of four adult books. *Boxy an Star* was ...listed for the *Guardian* First Book Award.

Praise for *Peter the Penguin Pioneer*

...hildren will laugh out loud at the zany ...ur and the witty one-liners . . . while David ... s' comical illustrations can't fail to raise a ...g le.' *Scholastic Literacy Time Plus Magazine*

'King is very good at making children think about their world . . . hugely inventive and charmingly funny, early readers will adore having this book read to them and will love trying it themselves' *Literary Review*

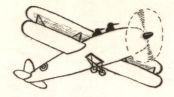

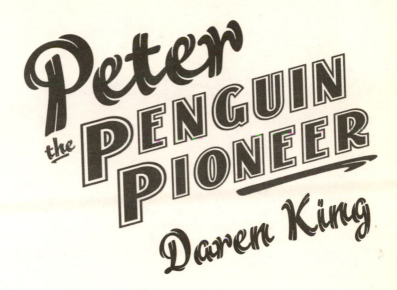

Peter the PENGUIN PIONEER

Daren King

Quercus

First published in Great Britain in 2008 by Quercus

This paperback edition published in 2009 by

Quercus
21 Bloomsbury Square
London
WC1A 2NS

A CIP catalogue reference for this book is available
from the British Library

ISBN 978 1 84724 832 9

This book is a work of fiction. Names, characters,
businesses, organizations, places and events are
either the product of the author's imagination
or are used fictitiously. Any resemblance to
actual persons, living or dead, events or
locales is entirely coincidental.

10 9 8 7 6 5 4 3 2 1

Printed and bound in Great Britain by Clays Ltd, St Ives plc.

To Rebecca, for the stripy jumper

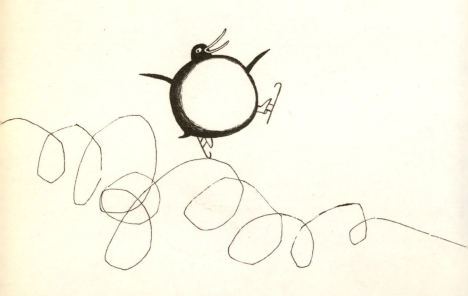

CONTENTS

Arrival

This book is for penguins only. If you're not a penguin, stop reading now or I'll slap you with my flippers.

Still reading?

That means you're a penguin!

I'm a penguin too. My name is Punky, and I'm a penguin. I have flippers, a beak, and, and, um, feet!

And I've got tufty ear feathers. They poke out. I'm the only penguin with tufty ear feathers.

Oh, and I'm an explorer! Just half an explorer really. The proper explorer is Peter. He's got a title. Peter's title is Peter the Penguin Pioneer. Exciting! And grand!

That's Peter over there, waddling through the snow to where the other penguins are cheering and waving their flippers.

And there, behind me, is Peter's aeroplane. Yes, an aeroplane!

Peter's aeroplane is a special type of aeroplane called a biplane. It's made of wood and it has two pairs of wings. Wings are like flippers but not as good because they can't slap. But they can fly! So they're better than flippers really.

Biplanes are ice cool!

We just flew back from the Jungle where we did an explore. We saw lions and tigers and, and, and, oh so many things, more things than I can count on one flipper.

Tigers are fierce. And stripy! They have

sharp tails and stripy teeth. No, that's not right. Stripy teeth and sharp tails. Or something like that.

This is Peter's luggage. I'm dragging it across the ice. It's heavy, I can't lift it, that's why I'm dragging it.

'Punky! Hurry up with that luggage.'

That was Peter.

I'm hurrying up as fast as I can, but the luggage is heavy and my flippers are tired.

I drag the luggage through the snow to where Peter is waiting, then I do a belly slide, just for fun. You would too if you had dragged the luggage!

One of the penguins picks me up with his flippers and carries me to the crowd of excited penguins, who lift me high above their beaks, shouting and cheering.

'Hooray for Punky!'

'Hooray for Peter the Penguin Pioneer!'

Peter opens the wooden trunk to present

the exotic gifts. We found them in the Jungle.
Ice cool!

'This is called a vine,' Peter says, passing
a long green wiggly thing to the excited
penguins.

'Wow!' the penguins say. 'How exotic!'

'And this is called a rock,' Peter says,
dumping the second exotic gift in the snow.

'The gifts are always the same,' one of the
penguins says. 'It's always rocks and vines.'

'And sticks,' one of the penguins says.

Peter silences the squabbling penguins by
holding up his flippers, then gives them this
ice-cool look, and says, 'I have saved the
most exotic gift until last.'

The penguins gasp. Ice cool!

'Punky and I have just returned from our
most dangerous explore yet. We ventured
deep into the Jungle, deeper than any
penguin has ever ventured before, and we
have returned with the tail of a leopard.'

Peter reaches into the trunk, pulls out exotic gift number three and drops it on to the snow, at the feet of a very clever penguin named Harold.

'It looks like another vine,' Harold says.

Peter looks up at the sky, at the falling snowflakes, then fixes his eyes on Harold. 'Leopard tails do look like vines, Harry.'

'Leopard tails do not have leaves,' Harold says. 'This, Peter, is a vine.'

Peter thinks for a moment, then says, 'Of course it's a vine. Any fool can see that.'

'But you said it was the tail of a leopard.'

'Perhaps I got the vine and the leopard tail mixed up.'

Harold looks down at the exotic gifts, shakes his beak.

'Never mind that,' Peter says. 'Punky and I are off on another explore. But first we must sleep. Come along, Punky.'

Exotic Artefacts

Peter's house is ice cool! It's got a door and, and, um, walls!

The house is full of exotic artefacts! Peter found the exotic artefacts in the Jungle. That was when I was still an egg.

I'm too tired to sleep, so I waddle about.

'Stop waddling about and get some rest,' Peter says. He lies down and goes to sleep.

Peter sleeps on the fur of a tiger! That's because he's a pioneer. I sleep on the icy floor, by the door. Peter says this is to keep the cold out.

The other penguins sleep out in the snow.

Just when I'm about to lie down and go to sleep, I hear a flipper-slap at the door. I poke my beak out to see who's there. It's Harold.

'Hello, Harold.'

'Let me in,' Harold says in a cross voice. 'I have to talk to Peter.'

'Peter is asleep,' I say, looking back at Peter's wobbling beak. 'If I wake him up he will tell me off.'

'If you don't wake him up,' Harold says, 'I will tell you off.'

I waddle up to Peter and peck him on the belly. Thawed out!

'Punky, if this isn't a dream, I will slap you with my flipper.'

'It is a dream,' I say. 'Um, Harold's here.'

Peter sits up. 'Harold? What does he want?'

'He wants to come in.'

'He can't!'

Then, Harold comes in. 'Hello, Peter.'

Peter stands up and starts waddling about.

'I've always wanted to see inside your house,' Harold says, looking at the exotic artefacts.

Peter scratches his beak, says nothing.

'The other penguins are concerned about the leopard's tail,' Harold says. 'They started to ask questions. Is Peter really a pioneer? Does he really sleep on the fur of a tiger? And is it true that Peter's house is full of exotic artefacts from the deepest corners of the Jungle?'

'It's true!' I say. 'Look!'

Harold waddles about, poking exotic artefacts with his beak. 'What's this?'

'That, Harold, is the tusk of an elephant.'

'It looks like an umbrella.'

'What's an umbrella?' I say.

'Persons use them to keep the rain off their beaks,' Harold says.

'What's rain?'

But Harold doesn't answer. 'Um, and this?'

'That, Harry, is a stuffed parrot.'

'It looks like a training shoe.'

'What's a training shoe?' I say.

'Persons wear them on their feet,' Harold says.

'But why?'

Harold doesn't answer. 'And what is this?'

'That,' Peter says, 'is the fur of a tiger. It's soft and it has stripes.'

Harold looks down at the tiger fur, shakes his beak.

'I killed the tiger myself,' Peter says. 'I slapped it about and pecked it with my beak.'

'It looks like a woolly jumper.'

'Tiger furs do look like woolly jumpers, Harry.'

I hold up my flippers to make myself tall. 'Harold! What's a woolly jumper?'

But Harold doesn't reply. 'I've seen enough. I will go and tell the other penguins that Peter is not a pioneer but a fraud.'

'Harry, please don't.'

Harold waddles to the door.

'If you tell the penguins I'm ordinary, they will be unhappy.'

Harold stops mid-waddle. 'Unhappy?'

'Penguins need pioneers, Harry, like they need fish and, um, more fish. The penguins need a hero, and that hero is me.'

Harold narrows his eyes, then waddles out into the snow.

IMPOSTORS!

After the sleep, we waddle out into the snow, and Peter slaps Harold on the shoulder. 'Did you tell them I'm a fraud, Harry?'

But then the penguins start to cheer and clap their flippers. 'Hooray for Punky! Hooray for Peter the Penguin Pioneer!'

Harold laughs. 'Ho ho!'

'Never mind that,' Peter says. 'What has been happening while me and Punky were in the Jungle?'

'It snowed,' one of the penguins says.

'Then it snowed again,' another penguin says.

'Anything else?'

'We went ice skating. It wasn't much fun because the Penguin Skating Rink is shrinking.'

'Shrinking?'

'Yes,' the penguin says. 'Come and see.'

We follow the penguin through the snow to the Penguin Skating Rink, and I do a belly slide, and one of the penguins eats a fish.

'It looks the same size as before,' Peter says.

'There used to be room to skate in circles,' one of the penguins says, 'but now it's too crowded.'

Peter scratches his beak with his flipper. He thinks for a moment, then tells the penguins to waddle on to the Penguin Skating Rink and waddle about.

I wait by the side with Harold and Peter.
Ice cool!

'Hmm,' Peter says. 'It does look crowded.'

I hold up my flippers to make myself tall.
'I know! I know! We can measure it.'

'Good thinking, Punky,' Harold says.
'Everyone off!'

We wait while the penguins waddle away,
then Peter says, 'How big was it before,
Punky?'

'It was two belly slides and a waddle.
Look at the size now.' I leap on to the ice, do
a belly slide, then another belly slide, then
waddle across to the far end. Then, I waddle
back to Harold and Peter.

Harold nods his beak. 'Two belly slides
and a waddle, the same size as before.'

'Perhaps there is a polar bear asleep on
the ice,' Peter says. 'Polar bears take up a lot
of room.'

Harold shakes his beak. 'We would be

able to see it.'

'Camouflage,' Peter says cleverly.

That means when something looks like something else, so it can hide. Snow is white so that it can hide on polar bears.

Harold slaps his flippers together. 'Everyone on to the ice. If you see a polar bear, report back to me.'

We all waddle on to the Penguin Skating Rink and waddle about. Ice cool! But no polar bears are found.

'Perhaps we've all got fatter,' one of the penguins says. 'Last week, I ate three fish, and then I ate another fish, and then I ate five more fish. Then, I ate a fish. Then I had a slap-up fish supper.'

'You had fish for pudding too,' another penguin says.

'Yes,' the first penguin says. 'Tasty!'

Peter shakes his beak. 'If we had all got fatter, our trousers wouldn't fit.'

'We don't wear trousers,' Harold says.
'We're penguins.'

Peter and Harold are about to give up
when I have an idea. 'Perhaps there are
more of us than before.'

'Of course,' Harold says. 'Let's do a
penguin belly count. Everyone line up.'

We all shuffle into a line, and Harold
walks along the line, slapping our bellies
with his flipper.

'One, two, three,' he counts, slap-slap-slap. 'Thirty-seven, thirty-eight, thirty-nine, and myself makes forty.'

'How many were there before?' Peter says.

'Twenty,' Harold says. 'There were twenty, and now there are forty.'

'There can't be, Harry. There aren't forty penguins in the entire world. At least, I don't think so.'

'Then there is only one explanation,' Harold says. 'The new penguins are not penguins at all. The twenty newcomers are impostors!'

Penguin impostors! Yay!

I've just done a belly slide. Did you see? Watch, I'll do it again.

Yay!

'Punky,' Peter says. 'Stop that.'

I look down at my feet.

'While you were sliding about like an ice cube, Harold and I were discussing the impostor problem, and we have a plan. Harold will design a series of tests to identify the penguin impostors.'

'Me?'

'It was your idea, Harry.'

Harold narrows his eyes. 'And what will you be doing while I test the penguins?'

'I will be in the Jungle with Punky.'

I do a belly slide. Yay!

Harold shakes his beak. 'You're the hero, Peter. You should be the penguin to identify the impostors. Unless, of course, you're a fraud.'

Peter looks up at the sky, at the falling snowflakes, then looks back at Harold. 'Leave it to me. I may be a lot of things, Harry, but I'm no fraud.'

FISH BEAK CATCH

'I'm hungry,' I say, waddling about. 'I want to eat a fish.'

'How about a fish sandwich? Yes, that's what I fancy. A fish sandwich.'

Harold doesn't say anything.

'I suppose you're wondering what a fish sandwich is, Harry.'

Harold narrows his eyes.

Peter looks up at the sky, at the falling snowflakes, then looks back at Harold. 'Ask me what a fish sandwich is, Harry.'

Harold shakes his beak.

I shake my beak, too. Thawed out!

'Do you know what you are, Peter?' Harold says, folding his flippers. 'A show-off.'

'Not true, Harry.'

'You've travelled the world in that tatty biplane of yours, and you want everyone to know it. The only reason you want a fish sandwich is because you know what they are and the rest of us don't.'

Peter doesn't say anything.

'All right,' Harold says. 'I give up. What, Peter, is a fish sandwich?'

Peter smiles a beaky penguin smile. 'A fish sandwich, Harold, is a fish between two, um, fish. I think.'

'A fish between two fish?'

'I think that's right, Harry.'

'And how is this fish sandwich put together?'

'You take a fish,' Peter says, 'and you

place a fish on top of it, and then you put another fish on top of that.'

Harold laughs. 'Ridiculous!'

'Or you insert the third fish between the first two.'

I do a belly slide, to get Peter to look at me, but he doesn't, so I do another belly slide and bump into Peter's feet.

'Punky, what are you doing?'

'I want a fish sandwich!'

Harold slaps me on the belly with his flipper. 'Then a fish sandwich you shall have.'

We waddle over to the hole in the ice, and Peter dives into the icy water and comes back holding a fish in his beak. He drops the fish on to the snow and dives for more fish. Ice cool!

'How many fish do we need, Punky?' Harold says. 'Three fish sandwiches, three fish for each sandwich.'

I count on my flippers. 'Um. Two.'

'You must learn to count properly,' Harold says. 'If you count on your flippers you can only count up to two. What if you need to count more than two?'

'I count on my feet.'

My feet are orange. Have you got orange feet? Of course you have, you're a penguin. If your feet aren't orange, stop reading this book!

'Yes?' Harold says.

I count on my feet. 'Still only two.'

'Wrong,' Harold says. 'To make three fish sandwiches, we need nine fish. How many do we have so far?'

I look at the heap of fish. 'Six.'

Peter pops out of the hole with another fish.

'Two more should do it,' Harold tells Peter.

Peter dives for two more fish, then we sit

in the snow and make fish sandwiches. Ice cool!

'What a delicious recipe,' Harold says. 'You can really taste the fish.'

'What's for pudding?' I say.

'You haven't finished your sandwich,' Peter says.

'I'm full.'

'If you're full,' Peter says, 'how can you have room for pudding?'

I point to my tummy with my flipper. 'I saved some space.'

Harold and Peter laugh.

'My turn,' Harold says, and he waddles to the edge of the hole in the ice.

'I'm the best swimmer,' Peter says. 'You wait here with Punky.' And he dives into the blue water.

'Peter is a show-off,' I say, folding my flippers.

'You're a show-off too, Punky.'

'Oh.'

'Why else would you keep sliding about?'

I look up at the sky, like Peter does when Harold tells him off.

When Peter is finished, there's a heap of fish as big as a big heap of fish, and they're all flapping about.

'Here,' Peter says to Harold. 'Catch!' He slaps a fish with his flipper, and it flies up into the air, and Harold catches it in his beak.

'Tasty,' Harold says.

I slap a fish with my flipper, but my flipper isn't as big as Peter's, so the fish doesn't fly up into the air. The fish gives me a mean look and flaps about.

'Try again,' Harold says. 'Like this.' He slaps a fish with his flipper, and it flies through the snowy sky and hits a sleeping polar bear on the head. The polar bear wakes up, looks over at Harold, lowers its head and goes back to sleep.

Peter laughs. 'Now who's the show-off?'

'Wait,' I say. 'Don't eat all the fish! We can use the fish to test a penguin.'

Peter looks at Harold, and Harold looks at Peter.

'Explain,' Peter says.

'We throw the fish at the penguin, and if the penguin catches the fish, the penguin is a penguin, and if the fish catches the penguin, the penguin is a fish.'

'That can't be right,' Harold says. 'You mean that if the penguin catches the fish, the penguin is a penguin, and if the penguin doesn't catch the fish, the penguin is an impostor.'

'Yes,' I say. 'That's right.'

Peter hugs me with his flipper. 'Well done, Punky. I was about to think of this idea myself, but I decided to let you think of it first.'

'How noble,' Harold says, narrowing his eyes.

'The test needs a name,' Peter says.

Harold looks at me. 'Punky?'

I try to do a belly slide but I'm too full. 'It's called the Fish Beak Catch.'

'Perfect,' Harold says. 'Now all we need is a penguin.'

'There's one,' I say, pointing with my flipper.

Peter grabs a fish with his beak and throws it at the penguin.

Harold holds his breath.

The penguin watches as the fish flies through the snowy sky. Then, just as the fish is about to fly over the penguin's head, the penguin opens its beak and catches the fish by the tail.

'There's three more penguins,' I say, pointing with my flipper.

Peter picks up a fish and throws it at the three penguins. They don't catch the fish!

'They may not have seen it,' Harold says. 'Throw another.'

Peter throws another fish. It flies over the beaks of the three penguins and disappears into the snow.

'Perhaps they just aren't hungry,' Harold says.

'But they're liars! They didn't catch the fish!'

Harold shakes his beak. 'Perhaps they didn't want to catch the fish, Punky.'

I grab a fish with my flipper. 'Let me try! It was my idea.'

'It won't work,' Harold says.

I throw the fish at the penguins. It hits one of them on the beak, and the beak falls off!

Not a real beak!

Liar!

Harold claps his flippers. 'Ho ho! The Fish Beak Catch is a success.'

'Slap it with your flipper,' Peter says. 'If it's a penguin, it will waddle about.'

We waddle up to the impostor, and Harold slaps it with his flipper. The impostor doesn't waddle about.

'Its feet have frozen to the ice,' Peter says. 'Penguin feet don't do that. Whatever this creature is, it is not a penguin.'

'Leave me alone!' the impostor says in a silly, speeded-up voice.

Peter looks the impostor up and down. 'Why have your feet frozen to the ice?'

'I stood still too long. And these aren't feet, they're claws.'

Harold picks up the wooden beak. 'This beak is false,' he says. 'It is carved from wood and painted orange.'

A false beak! The beak is a liar!

'What are you?' Peter says.

'A penguin,' the impostor says. 'Leave me alone!'

'You might as well tell the truth,' Peter says. 'You can't get away. You're stuck.'

'What about the flippers?' Harold says. 'Are the flippers false too?'

'Almost certainly,' Peter says. 'Right,' he tells the impostor. 'Those false flippers aren't fooling anyone. Let's have them!'

The impostor wriggles out of the flippers and drops them on to the snow.

'What we have here,' Peter says, looking

at the false flippers, 'is a type of person-
clothing called a dinner jacket. And that
floppy thing is called a bow tie. The white
thing is called a shirt.'

The impostor takes off the bow tie and
shirt, and drops them on to the dinner jacket.
Thawed out!

Harold laughs. 'What a ridiculous
creature.'

'It's covered in brown hair,' Peter says.

'And what's that round the back? There's a big fluffy thing poking out of its bottom.'

'Stop it!' the impostor says in a silly, speeded-up voice. 'That's my tail. Leave it alone.'

'What kind of animal are you?' Peter asks.

'I'm a squirrel. Leave me alone!'

Peter scratches his beak with his flipper.

'A squiggle? What's a squiggle?'

'I didn't say squiggle. I said squirrel.

Leave me alone or I'll gnaw you.'

'If we set you free,' Peter says, putting his flipper around the squiggle's shoulder, 'do you promise to scamper off, back to wherever you came from?'

'I promise,' the squiggle says. 'Hurry, before my claws turn blue.'

We breathe warm air on to the squiggle's claws. Penguin breath is warm and cosy. The squiggle pulls itself free from the ice, then scampers off across the snow.

Hazelnut Glance

'This,' Harold says, putting on the false flippers, 'is the official impostor test jacket.'

A penguin with false flippers! Ice cool!

'Wear it with pride,' Peter says.

'Oh,' Harold says, 'I have found something in the pockets.'

'What are pockets?' I say.

Peter points to two square things, one on either side of the jacket. 'Persons put things in them, then take them out again.'

'But why?' Harold says.

'Um. I don't know.'

Harold takes the things out of the pockets and shows them to Peter. 'Brown things,' Harold says. 'I wonder what they are.'

'I've seen these before,' Peter says. 'They're a type of nut.'

'A type of nut,' Harold says, rolling the brown things in his flipper.

'Yes,' Peter says. 'I remember now. They're hazelnuts. Squiggles eat them.'

'So hazelnuts are a type of nut,' Harold says, 'and nuts are a type of fish.'

Peter shakes his beak. 'They're not a type of fish, but they are food. Fish are not the only food, Harold.'

'Fish are the only food for me,' Harold says.

'And me,' I say.

'Let's eat some,' Harold says.

'Yes,' I say. 'Let's eat some fish.'

I like fish. Do you like fish? Of course
you do, you're a penguin. Well, you'd better
be. If you're not a penguin, stop reading
this book!

'I didn't mean let's eat fish,' Harold
says. 'I meant let's eat the hazelnuts.'

'Penguins can't eat hazelnuts,' Peter
says. 'They're too hard. You'll hurt your
beak.'

'If squiggles can eat them, penguins can
eat them.' Harold flings a hazelnut into his
beak and bites. 'Ouch!'

'Squiggles gnaw them with their teeth,'
Peter says. 'If you haven't got teeth, you
can't eat nuts.'

Harold spits the hazelnut on to the snow.
'I shall throw them away.'

'Wait,' I say. 'Don't throw the hazelnuts
away! I have an idea.'

'Not another one,' Peter says.

'We can use the hazelnuts to test the

penguins.'

'Ridiculous!' Harold says. 'You can't test penguins with hazelnuts. Penguins don't even like hazelnuts.'

'Harold is right,' Peter says.

'That's how the test works,' I say. 'We ask a penguin if it likes hazelnuts, and if the penguin says it does like hazelnuts, the penguin is a squiggle.'

Harold shakes his beak. 'Squiggles disguised as penguins do not discuss their eating habits, Punky.'

'I don't mean that we *ask* them.'

'Then what do you mean?'

I look at my orange feet, and the snow. 'Um.'

'Yes?'

'We roll a hazelnut past the penguin, and if the hazelnut glances at the penguin, the hazelnut is an impostor.'

Peter looks at Harold, and Harold looks at Peter.

'That can't be right,' Harold says. 'You mean that if the penguin glances at the hazelnut, the penguin is an impostor.'

'Yes,' I say. And then I slide on my belly. Yay!

You can do it too. Yay!

'Punky, stop that,' Peter says in a cross voice. 'Help choose a penguin for the test.'

I look around at the penguins. 'There are too many to choose from.'

'Thirty-nine, by my calculation,' Harold says. 'That includes us three. Twenty penguins and nineteen penguin impostors.'

'Did you just work that out, Harry, or did you do a quick belly count?'

'I worked it out, Peter.'

'Clever.'

'Yes, I am clever,' Harold says.

Peter looks up at the sky, at the falling snowflakes, then back at Harold. 'I bet you can't fly a plane, Harry.'

'I don't want to fly a plane. If penguins were meant to fly, Peter, we would have wings.'

'We do have wings,' Peter says, waggling his flippers.

'Flippers aren't wings,' Harold says.

Peter looks back at the biplane. '*That* has wings,' he says proudly.

'Yes,' Harold says, 'and they look like they're about to fall off.'

'There's a penguin!' I say, pointing with my flipper. 'It's on the Penguin Skating Rink. You can't roll hazelnuts in the snow. They won't roll.'

'Good point,' Harold says.

'I was about to think of that myself,' Peter says.

Harold narrows his eyes. 'And I suppose you were about to invent Punky's hazelnut test. Am I right?'

'Actually, Harry, I invented the hazelnut test many years ago in the Jungle. I call it the Hazelnut Glance.'

Harold folds his flippers. 'Oh yes?'

'A gorilla was hiding behind a tree, but I was not sure which tree. I rolled a hazelnut along the ground. The gorilla poked its head out from behind the tree to glance at the hazelnut, and I made my escape.'

'And did the gorilla eat the hazelnut?'

'Of course,' Peter says. 'Gorillas love

hazelnuts.'

Harold looks down at the snow, shakes his beak.

'Never mind that,' Peter says. 'Let's get on with the test, before the penguin waddles off and eats a fish.'

'I'll roll the hazelnut,' Harold says. 'You two watch for the glance.'

Harold takes the hazelnut out of his pocket and rolls it on to the Penguin Skating Rink, right in front of the penguin. 'Did the penguin glance?'

'I don't think so,' I say.

'Did you see a glance, Peter?'

Peter shakes his beak. 'That penguin did not glance at the hazelnut. Try another penguin.'

'There's another two,' I say, pointing with my flipper. 'And one of them looks a bit funny.'

'Here we go,' Harold says. And he rolls

another hazelnut on to the ice.

'There!' Peter says. 'The penguin on the left glanced at the hazelnut.'

'Did you see a glance, Punky?'

'No,' I say. 'I was looking at my feet. Why are they orange?'

'This is not the time for daft questions,' Harold says. 'We have an impostor to unmask.'

'Leave this to me,' Peter says, and off he waddles.

'Peter said it was the one on the left,' Harold says. 'The one that looks a bit funny.'

'I bet it's another squiggle, Harold.'

'He's going to waggle the

beak.'

'It's not even a real beak,' I say, pointing
with my flipper.

Peter takes hold of the penguin's beak
and waggles it till it falls off.

POLAR BEAR HUG

'Harold,' I say, 'do you remember when you slapped the fish with your flipper?'

'Yes,' Harold says, 'I do remember that.'

'It flew up into the air. Do you remember?'

Harold nods his beak.

'It hit a polar bear on the head.'

Harold laughs. 'Ho ho!'

'The polar bear was asleep. Do you remember?'

'I do remember, yes.'

'You woke it up.'

'And what a way to wake up!'

'It gave you a mean look, then went back to sleep.'

'Punky, my memory of this event is as clear as icicles. What are you trying to say?'

I point with my flipper. 'The polar bear is right behind you.'

Harold looks over his shoulder. When he sees the huge polar bear, he yelps in terror and waddles off.

The polar bear just stands there with her paws on her hips, shaking her head. 'That penguin woke me up. I think I will eat him.'

'You can't eat Harold,' Peter says. 'He's our friend.'

'He won't be your friend if I eat him.'

'My name is Punky,' I say to the polar bear. 'This is Peter, the Penguin Pioneer. What's your name?'

'Denise,' the polar bear says. 'When your

friend Harold comes back, tell him I want to eat him.'

'Polar bears don't eat penguins,' Peter says. 'Polar bears eat fish.'

'There aren't any fish left. You penguins keep eating them.'

'There's plenty under the ice,' Peter says.

Just then, Harold comes back. He's not wearing the official impostor test jacket. He took it off!

'Hello, polar bear,' Harold says. 'I'm not the penguin who threw the fish. That was Harold. My name is Henry.'

'You can't fool me,' Denise says. 'You're Harold.'

Harold laughs. 'Harold wears a jacket. I'm not wearing a jacket.'

'You took it off,' Denise says.

Harold looks at Peter and me. 'Tell her my name is Henry.'

'His name is Harold,' I say, jumping up

and down. 'He's a liar!'

Harold narrows his eyes. 'Thanks, Punky.'

Denise opens her jagged mouth and grabs
Harold with her paws, but Harold shoots up
into the air and vanishes into the falling
snow.

Denise looks confused. 'Where did he go?'

'Penguins are slippery,' Peter tells her. 'He
slipped out of your paws like a bar of soap.'

'What's a bar of soap?'

'Persons use them to make their faces
pink,' Peter says. 'Um, I think.'

'I want to eat Harold,' Denise says, and
lumbers off into the snow.

Lumbers is what polar bears do when they
move about. Do you move like that? If you
do, you're a polar bear. Stop reading this
book!

'Punky, I admire your honesty,' Peter
says, 'but there are times when it is better to
tell a fib. Harold could have been eaten.'

'But he lied!'

Peter looks down at the snow, shakes his beak.

'Look!' I say, pointing with my flipper. 'Harold!'

'He's put the jacket back on,' Peter says. 'I should be wearing that jacket.'

Harold waddles towards us through the snow.

'Punky,' Harold says in a cross voice, 'you could have got me eaten. I'm all for honesty but not when there are hungry polar bears about.'

I look at my orange feet. 'Sorry,' I say, thinking about my feet, wondering why they are orange.

'The polar bear has gone now,' Peter says.

'I hope she comes back,' I say. 'I have an idea.'

Peter shakes his beak. 'Not another one.'

'Polar bears can test penguins! The polar bear hugs the penguin. If the penguin shoots up into the air, the penguin is a polar bear.'

Peter looks at Harold, and Harold looks at Peter.

'That can't be right,' Harold says. 'You mean that if the penguin shoots up into the air, the penguin is a penguin.'

'Yes,' I say. And then I slide on my belly. Yay!

'Stop that,' Peter says.

'Let him slide about,' Harold says. 'A penguin deserves a belly slide after having such a good idea.'

Peter looks up at the sky, at the falling snowflakes, then fixes his eyes on Harold. 'That was my idea, Harry. I thought of it just before Punky thought of it.'

Harold narrows his eyes.

'I'm telling you the truth, Harry. I call it the Polar Bear Hug.'

'That wasn't a hug,' Harold says. 'Denise wanted to eat me. If this idea is going to work, we need to prevent Denise from eating the penguins.'

'That's easy,' Peter says. 'We give her some fish.'

'You two can give the fish to Denise,' Harold says. 'If she sees me, she will eat me.'

'Take off the jacket,' Peter laughs, 'and she won't recognise you.'

Peter and Harold dive through the hole in the ice and catch fish and drop them on to the snow. The fish heap gets bigger and bigger and bigger. Ice cool! Then, when the fish heap is as big as an even bigger heap of fish, Harold and Peter stop diving for fish.

'That should do it,' Harold says.

'If Denise can eat all these,' Peter says, 'I will eat my hat.'

'You don't wear a hat,' Harold says.

'In that case,' Peter says, 'I'll eat my flying goggles.'

Harold laughs. 'Ho ho!'

We wait for Denise to lumber over, then Peter turns to Harold to ask him something, but Harold has waddled off. Thawed out!

'Your friend keeps running away,' Denise says.

'He's busy,' Peter says. 'If you want to talk to Harold, you will have to make an appointment.'

I don't know what appointment means. Do you? I hope it's a type of fish. Fish are ice cool!

'I only wanted to eat him.'

'Don't eat Harold,' I say. 'Eat the fish!'

Denise looks down at the big heap of fish. 'Are these for me?'

'If you promise not to eat Harold,' Peter says, 'and you agree to help us.'

Just then, Harold comes back, still
wearing the official impostor test jacket.
'I've decided to give myself up,' Harold

says, holding his flippers above his head.

'Denise doesn't want to eat you,' Peter
says. 'She has decided to help us instead.'

Harold narrows his eyes. 'How noble.'

'Right!' Denise says, rubbing her paws

together. 'What do you want me to do?'

'Hug a penguin,' Peter says.

'Then I can eat the fish?'

'Here comes a penguin now,' Harold says.

Denise waits for the penguin to waddle
past, then grabs it from behind, squeezing it
with her big white paws. The penguin shoots
up into the air like a bar of soap. Ice cool!

'The genuine article,' Harold says. 'Try
those two.'

Denise nods her big snowy head. She

lumbers up to the two penguins and hugs them, one with her left paw and one with her right.

The penguins don't shoot up into the air! Impostors!

Peter waddles through the snow to the penguins and waggles the wooden beaks till they fall off.

The penguins are liars!

Denise opens her big fluffy arms and the two squiggles scamper off into the snow.

'They won't return in a hurry,' Harold says. 'Not without false wooden beaks.'

'Hug one more penguin,' Peter tells Denise, 'then you can eat as many fish as you like.'

'That one,' I say, pointing to a penguin who looks a bit funny.

'Wait till it waddles past,' Peter says.

We stand in a row, Denise, Harold, Peter and me, and Peter whistles a frosty tune. The penguin waddles past, and Denise clamps it in her big white paws.

The penguin doesn't shoot up into the air.

Another impostor. Thawed out!

Peter is just about to unmask the impostor when I slap Peter's belly with my flipper. 'Let me do it! Let me do it!'

'You won't be able to reach, Punky. You're too small.'

'I'm not small. I'm medium!' I jump up and slap the false wooden beak until it falls off.

I unmasked a squiggle. Ice cool!

'Let it scamper away,' Peter tells Denise.

Denise lets go of the squiggle, but it doesn't scamper away. It scampers up a nearby flagpole and sits on top!

Harold scratches his beak. 'Such odd behaviour.'

FLAGPOLE SCAMPER

Denise has eaten all the fish. Thawed out!

We watch Denise lie down in the snow and rub her big fluffy tummy.

'Yet more odd behaviour,' Harold says, waddling about and flapping his flippers. 'Are penguins the only animals who are normal?'

'Punky and I have travelled far and wide,' Peter says, 'and I can tell you, penguins are the only normal animals in the entire world.'

Harold looks at me. 'Do you agree, Punky?'

I don't say anything. I'm looking at the flagpole.

Harold waddles over.

'Harold,' I say, 'why are flagpoles?'

'Why are flagpoles what?'

'Flagpoles.'

'Why are flagpoles flagpoles?'

'Why are flagpoles?'

'Why *are* they?'

'Yes.'

'Why are they what?' Harold shakes his beak, waddles back to Peter. 'Are you sure penguins are normal, Peter?'

'Never mind that, Harry. The Penguin Skating Rink is still crowded. We need to unmask another impostor.'

'There can't be many left,' Harold says. 'Let's think. We unmasked one with the Fish Beak Catch and one with the Hazelnut

Glance. Denise caught another three with the Polar Bear Hug. How many is that, Punky?'

'Two,' I say, counting on my flippers.

'Wrong,' Harold says. 'Try counting on your flippers, your feet and your beak.'

'Um. Five?'

'Five,' Harold says. 'How many does that leave, Peter?'

Peter makes a row of peck marks in the snow with his beak. 'Twenty peck marks,' he says, 'for twenty penguin impostors. Waddle about on five. You can do that, Punky.'

I waddle about on five of Peter's peck marks.

'Now count the peck marks you didn't waddle about on. Harry?'

'One, two, three,' Harold says, counting peck marks, the ones I didn't waddle about on. 'More than ten.'

'Fifteen,' Peter says, 'I think.'

Harold nods his beak. 'Fifteen. That's still a lot of impostors.'

'This explains why the Penguin Skating Rink is still crowded,' Peter says. 'We need a new impostor test.'

'I've thought of one,' I say, holding up my flippers to make myself tall.

'So have I,' Peter says.

Harold looks at Peter. 'Go on.'

'Punky can tell you his idea first,' Peter says.

Harold smiles a beaky penguin smile. 'No,' he says. 'You tell us your idea, then we will hear from Punky.'

'I am a gentleman penguin,' Peter says, waddling to the side. 'A gentleman penguin always allows a penguin with tufty ears to go first.'

'How do we know you're not going to copy Punky's idea?'

'I wouldn't do that, Harry.'

'Prove it.'

Peter looks up at the sky, at the falling snowflakes, then fixes his eyes on Harold. 'I haven't got an idea, Harry.'

'You haven't got an idea?'

Peter shakes his beak. 'No.'

'You were going to copy Punky's idea.'

'Don't tell anyone. I'm a pioneer, Harry. I'm supposed to be heroic.'

'You can fly a plane. That's heroic.'

'Yes,' Peter says. 'Flying a plane is heroic.'

'Then bury your ego and let Punky tell us his idea.'

What's an ego? I hope it's a type of fish!

'What's your idea, Punky?' Harold says.

'You remember when the squiggle scampered up the flagpole? We can use that to test the penguins.'

Peter looks at Harold, and Harold looks at Peter.

'Ridiculous!' Harold says. 'You can't test

penguins with flagpoles. Penguins have no interest in flagpoles. And penguins can't scamper.'

'Harold is right,' Peter says.

'That's how the test works. We tell the penguin to scamper up the flagpole, and if the penguin scampers up the flagpole, the flagpole is an impostor.'

Harold scratches his beak. 'Are you sure you got that right?'

'Um.' I look down at my orange feet. 'No.'

'You mean that if the penguin scampers up the flagpole, the penguin is an impostor.'

'Yes,' I say. 'That's right.'

'But what if the penguin doesn't want to scamper up the flagpole?'

'Then the penguin is a penguin.'

Harold shakes his beak. 'It might be a squiggle who doesn't like being told what to do.'

'I don't mean that we *tell* it.'

'Then what *do* you mean?' Harold says.

I look at my orange feet, and the snow. 'Um.'

'Yes?'

'We chase it.'

'Penguins don't waddle away from other penguins,' Harold says.

Peter has an idea. 'Perhaps the polar bears can help. Look, there's Denise.'

We wait until Denise lumbers over, then we tell her the plan.

'I don't feel like chasing penguins,' Denise says.

'What if we give you some fish?'

Denise rubs her fat tummy. 'I'm full.'

'What about your friends?' Peter says. 'Perhaps your friends would like some fish.'

Denise taps a mound of snow on the shoulder, and the mound of snow yawns and sits up. Another polar bear! Thawed out!

'Are you hungry, Pauline?'

'Denise, I'm starving,' the sleepy polar bear says.

'These penguins will get you some fish. But first, you have to chase a penguin.'

'Why do they want me to do that?'

Denise shrugs her snowy shoulders.

'Sometimes I wonder,' Pauline says, 'if polar bears are the only normal animals in the entire world.'

'Never mind that,' Harold says. 'Will you help?'

'I will if Tracy will,' Pauline says. 'Tracy, are you hungry?'

'Pauline, I'm starving,' a mound of snow says. The mound of snow sits up, yawns, and rubs its big sleepy eyes.

The mound of snow is another polar bear! Ice cool!

Pauline tells Tracy about the plan, then turns to Harold. 'Start running, Harold, and

we will chase you.'

'Not me,'
Harold says.

'Punky will
choose one,' Peter
says. 'Punky?'

I waddle round
in a circle, looking
for a penguin, one
who looks a bit
funny. 'There's
one!'

'You two go,'
Denise says. 'I'm
full.'

'Don't harm it,'
Peter says. 'Just
chase it up the
flagpole.'

We watch
Pauline and Tracy

waddle off through the snow. The moment it sees the two polar bears, it drops its wooden beak and scampers to the top of the flagpole.

Harold picks up the wooden beak and puts it in his pocket. 'I'll keep hold of these.'

'Here comes another penguin,' Peter says.

The penguin waddles over to the flagpole, looks up at the squiggle perched on top, and scratches its beak with a flipper. Ice cool!

Peter slaps Pauline on the tummy. 'Go!'

When the penguin sees Pauline lumbering about in the snow, it holds up its flippers, circles the flagpole twice, and waddles off.

'It didn't scamper up the flagpole,' Peter says.

'The penguin must be a penguin,' Harold says. 'A squiggle would have scampered up the flagpole to join its friend.'

'This is fun,' Pauline says. 'I want to chase more penguins.'

'Let's try a different flagpole,' Peter says.

We find another flagpole, and Pauline and Tracy chase more penguins. Most of the penguins waddle away, but three scamper up the flagpole, dropping their wooden beaks in the snow.

Harold picks up the wooden beaks and puts them into his pocket. Ice cool!

'I like this test,' Peter says. 'It needs a name.'

'It already has a name,' I say.

'Wait,' Peter says. 'I'm thinking.'

'It's called the Flagpole Scamper,' I say, holding up my flippers to make myself tall.

Peter looks up at the sky, at the falling snowflakes. He opens his beak to speak, but then he closes it again and doesn't say anything.

'What about our fish?' Pauline says. 'We're starving.'

'Peter will catch your fish,' Harold says. 'Peter is the best swimmer.'

Peter waddles off to the hole in the ice, the three polar bears lumbering behind, Denise rubbing her full tummy.

Harold looks at me. 'How best to use the time?'

'We can slide about!'

'And what would that achieve?'

'Fun,' I say, sliding on my belly. Yay!

Can you slide about? If you can't, you're not a penguin, and you're not allowed to read this book.

I waddle up a snowy hill and slide down towards Harold. Harold waddles out of the way. 'It does look fun,' Harold says. 'Though not terribly productive.'

'That's why it's fun, Harold. You should have a go.'

'Not now, Punky. We have to deal with these impostors.'

'How many did we get with the Flagpole Scamper?'

'I forget.'

'Count the beaks.' I point at Harold's pocket with my flipper.

Harold counts the beaks, then puts them back into his pocket. 'Four false wooden beaks.'

'There can't be many impostors left, Harold.'

Harold makes fifteen waddle marks in the snow. 'Fifteen impostors minus the four we caught with the Flagpole Scamper.' Harold takes the four false wooden beaks from his pocket and pokes each beak into a waddle mark.

Waddle marks with beaks! Ice cool!

'Count the waddle marks without beaks,' Harold says. 'That will tell you how many impostors are left.'

I count the waddle marks, the ones without beaks. 'Eleven.'

'Eleven squiggles disguised as penguins,'

Harold says. 'No wonder the Penguin Skating Rink is still crowded. We need another impostor test. Oh, here comes Peter.'

Silly Snowman

'Pauline and Tracy only ate one fish each,' Peter says. 'I thought they would eat a hundred.'

'They must be on a diet,' Harold says.

Just then, something hits Peter on the back of the head.

Harold laughs. 'Ho ho!'

Peter rubs the back of his head with his flipper.

'Sorry to laugh,' Harold says, 'but the look on your beak was hilarious.'

Peter waddles round and examines the
snow for whatever hit him on the back of the
head. 'It's disappeared, Harry.'

'No,' I say, bending down. 'It's here.' I
point with my flipper. 'A round ball of snow.'

'A round ball of snow?' Harold says.
'Ridiculous!'

'An impostor threw it,' I say. 'Um, I think.'

Harold shakes his beak. 'Round snow! Whatever will they think of next?'

'I think it's called a snowball,' Peter says. 'Where did the impostor find it?'

'That,' Harold says, 'is a mystery.'

I hold up my flippers to make myself tall. 'I know! I know!'

'Yes?' Peter says.

'Yes?' Harold says.

I look down at my orange feet. 'I don't know.'

Harold narrows his eyes. 'Then why say you did?'

'I wanted to be clever.'

'You are clever, Punky. You have that pioneering spirit, like Peter.'

I smile a beaky penguin smile.

Can you smile a beaky penguin smile? If you can't, you're not a penguin. Stop reading this book!

'Think,' Harold tells me. 'Scratch your beak and think about snowballs.'

'And squiggles,' Peter says.

I scratch my beak and think about snowballs and squiggles. 'Oh! I've worked it out. The squiggle made the snowball. It picked up some snow and squished it.'

Peter looks at Harold, and Harold looks at Peter.

'Is that possible?' Harold says.

'Everything is possible,' Peter says, 'if you have that pioneering spirit.' He scoops up some snow with his flippers and squishes it into a snowball.

'It's not very round,' Harold says.

'You try, Harry.' Peter passes the snowball to Harold, but it falls apart.

'I prefer to use my own,' Harold says, and scoops up some more snow.

'Perhaps you need claws, Harry.'

'No,' Harold says. 'What you need is patience.'

Patience is a type of fish. Um, I think.

'Take off the official impostor test jacket,' Peter says. 'You can't make snowballs wearing a jacket.'

Harold narrows his eyes. 'You just want the jacket for yourself.'

'No thought could be further from my beak, Harry.'

Harold takes off the jacket and drops it on to the snow. He scoops up some more snow and squishes it into a snowball.

'Still not round, Harry.'

'Look!' I say, pointing with my flipper. 'An impostor! It might be the one who threw the snowball.'

'It might not be an impostor,' Harold says. 'It might be a penguin.'

'But it's funny looking.'

'Well, so are you,' Harold says. 'You've got tufty ear feathers.'

'Throw snowballs at it,' Peter says.

Harold throws the snowball, but it falls apart in the air.

Then, something funny happens. The impostor starts to laugh. It laughs so hard, its false wooden beak falls off. Ice cool!

'Punky was right, Harry. It is an impostor. And it's laughing at your snowball.'

'How rude,' Harold says, putting on the jacket. 'My snowball wasn't that bad.'

'It was, Harry.'

'The squiggle has scampered off,' I say, pointing with my flipper, 'and it left the false wooden beak.'

Harold waddles over to the beak, picks it

up and puts it into his pocket.

'This could be a new impostor test,' I say, holding up my flippers to make myself tall.

'Ridiculous!' Harold says. 'You can't test penguins by making them laugh till their beaks fall off.'

'Harold is right,' Peter says.

I jump up and down in the snow. 'But we just did!'

'I'm not making any more snowballs,' Harold says.

Peter looks up at the sky, at the falling snowflakes, then fixes his eyes on Harold. 'Harry, you don't have to. I have an idea.'

'Yes?'

'We make a snowman.'

Harold narrows his eyes. 'What's a snowman?'

'A snowman, Harry, is a person made of snow.'

'And what does it do?'

'It doesn't do anything. Snowmen are as pointless as flagpoles and, um, pockets.'

'And this snowman will make the impostors laugh until their beaks fall off?'

'If we make it silly enough, Harry.'

I hold up my flipper. 'Let's make the snowman on the ice. The impostors will see it when they ice skate.'

'Good idea,' Harold says.

And off we waddle to the Penguin Skating Rink.

'It still looks crowded,' Peter says. 'How many impostors left, Harry?'

'At the last count,' Harold says, 'there were eleven.'

'Eleven,' Peter says, nodding his beak.

'Minus one,' Harold says, taking a false wooden beak out of his pocket. 'This is the beak from the squiggle who laughed at the snowball.'

'That leaves ten,' Peter says.

'The snowman will have to be hilarious,'
Harold says, 'to unmask ten impostors.
How do we start?'

'We make a mound of snow,' Peter says,
'and pat it with our flippers until it looks
like a person.'

Peter and Harold scoop up big flipper-
loads of snow and carry them to the
Penguin Skating Rink, while penguins and
impostors skate around them in circles.

I don't help. Harold says my flippers are
too diddly.

'It needs a nose,' Peter says. 'Persons use
a carrot.'

'What's a carrot?' Harold says.

'I don't know, but it's pointy and orange.'

Harold takes the false wooden beak out of
his pocket and shows it to Peter. 'Like this?'

Peter takes the false wooden beak from
Harold and pokes it into the mound of snow.

'It doesn't look much like a person,'

Harold says.

I jump up and down, waving my flippers about. 'I know! I know! We forgot to do the patting.'

'He's right,' Harold says to Peter.

We pat the snow with our flippers, pat-pat-pat, and I slide around on my belly, and Harold eats a fish.

'That should do it,' Peter says.

Then we waddle to the edge of the ice and watch the penguins skate around the snowman.

'None of the penguins are laughing,' Harold says. 'Perhaps the snowman isn't silly enough. Perhaps it looks too much like a person.'

Peter looks at the snowman, shakes his beak. 'If persons look like that, Harry, I'll eat my flying goggles.'

'Would you like to see our snowman?' Harold asks one of the penguins. But the penguin just keeps on skating.

'That one looks a bit funny,' I say, pointing with my flipper, but the penguin has already skated past.

'Wait till it comes round again,' Peter says.

'There's another one,' I say, pointing with my flipper.

'Stop!' Harold shouts, and the penguin stops.

'What do you want?' the penguin says in a silly, speeded-up voice.

'We've made a snowman,' Harold says.

The penguin looks at the snowman. Nothing happens at first. Then, the penguin starts to laugh. It laughs so much, its false wooden beak falls off. Thawed out!

Harold picks up the beak and puts it into his pocket.

'This,' Peter says, 'is the best impostor test yet. And it was my idea.'

'Does it have a name, Peter?' Harold asks.

Peter looks up at the sky, at the falling snowflakes, then fixes his eyes on Harold. 'I am so proud of this test that I will let Punky choose the name.'

'How noble,' Harold says, narrowing his eyes. 'Punky?'

I scratch my beak with my flipper. 'We will call it the, um.'

'Yes?' Peter says.

'Yes?' Harold says.

'The Silly Snowman. Um, I think.'

'Perfect,' Harold says. 'Wait, something is happening.'

Two of the penguins are looking up at the snowman. One of them smiles. The other grins. Then, they both start to laugh.

'Grab the false wooden beaks,' Peter says.

'Wait,' Harold says. 'Let's see what happens.'

The penguins laugh and laugh and laugh. They laugh so hard, their false wooden beaks fall off.

Harold waddles over to the impostors, picks up the two false wooden beaks and puts them into his pocket. Thawed out!

I waddle up to Peter. 'Harold is clever,' I say.

'I should be wearing that jacket, Punky.'

'But that's Harold's jacket.'

Peter looks up at the sky, at the falling snowflakes, says nothing.

'I can hear more laughter,' I say, waving my flippers. 'It's coming from behind the snowman.'

We waddle round to the other side of the snowman. Three more penguins! And they look a bit funny!

The penguins are rolling about in the

snow, laughing, beating the snow with their claws.

Liars!

'Wait till their beaks fall off,' Peter says.

Harold waits till the false wooden beaks fall off, then puts them into his pocket.

'There can't be many impostors left,' Peter says.

Harold takes the beaks out of his pocket, counts. 'Six. And the snowman's nose makes seven.'

'I hope they have a sense of humour, Harry.'

'Look!' I say, pointing with my flippers. 'Another laughing impostor. Oh, and another!'

'There's one over here,' Harold says.

'And I can see one more,' Peter says.

Harold gathers up the false wooden beaks and puts them into his pocket. 'That's the lot. That's twenty.'

I slide on my belly. 'We've done it. Yay!'

And we all clap our flippers. Me, Harold and Peter.

'This jacket is getting heavy,' Harold says. 'I think I will take it off.'

Peter nods his beak, says nothing.

Harold takes off the official impostor test jacket, the pocket bulging with false wooden beaks, and drops it on to the snow.

'Hush!' Peter says. 'I heard laughter.'

'Where?'

'Behind the snowman, Harry.'

Harold waddles round the snowman, then keeps on waddling until he's back with Peter and me. 'There's nothing there.'

'There is, Harry. I heard it.'

Again, Harold waddles round the snowman. 'Peter, there are no impostors behind that snowman.'

'Have another look.'

Harold waddles round the snowman

three more times. He's so dizzy, he falls flat on his beak. Thawed out!

'Punky,' Peter says, 'help me put on the jacket.'

'But that's Harold's jacket, Peter.'

'It's what he would have wanted,' Peter says, wriggling his flippers into the sleeves. He takes the ten false wooden beaks out of

the pocket and drops them on to the snow. 'I'm a dapper flipper-flapper,' Peter says, looking at his reflection in the ice. 'You wait here with Harold. I have an announcement to make.'

I sit in the snow and wait for Harold to sit up.

'Where's Peter?' Harold asks, scratching his beak with his flipper.

'He's talking to the other penguins.'

Harold narrows his eyes. 'Where?'

I point with my flipper. 'Perhaps he's gone to tell them about the impostors.'

'I don't believe it! He's wearing my jacket!'

Departure

We waddle through the snow, Harold and me, and I do a belly slide, and Harold eats a fish.

'Hello, penguins,' Harold says. Three of the penguins pick Peter up and lift him high above their beaks, shouting and cheering.

'Our turn next,' Harold tells me.

We watch the penguins carry Peter across the snow, laughing and flipper-clapping.

'Here they come,' Harold says.

One of the penguins waddles towards us. 'Peter saved the Penguin Skating Rink.

He's our hero!'

Harold looks at me, and I look at Harold.

'The Penguin Skating Rink was shrinking,' the penguin tells us. 'Peter made it big again.'

Harold narrows his eyes. 'How heroic.'

'Is that really what happened?' I ask Harold.

Harold shakes his beak. 'Peter, I want a word.'

'Not now, Harry. I'm off to the Jungle. Come along, Punky.'

The penguins drop Peter on to the snow, and off he waddles. Thawed out!

Harold folds his flippers. 'Punky, I don't think you should go to the Jungle with Peter.'

'But why, Harold?'

'Most of the impostor tests were your idea, and Peter stole the glory.'

'I didn't want the glory,' I say. 'I just wanted to help.'

'He stole my jacket too. Punky, where are you going?'

'To the Jungle.'

And off I waddle through the snow.

When I reach the plane, Peter has already started the engine. It's noisy and the propeller spins round and round and round and I'm so excited I can hardly waddle.

'Up you come!'

I climb up to my seat and we put our goggles over our eyes and the wheels turn and the plane starts to move and the penguins are flapping their flippers and cheering and, um, we take off.

Up, up and away!

Ice cool!

But something bad happens. The engine stops making a noise, the propeller stops spinning, and the plane starts to go down.

'Cover your beak!' Peter shouts. 'We're going to crash land!'

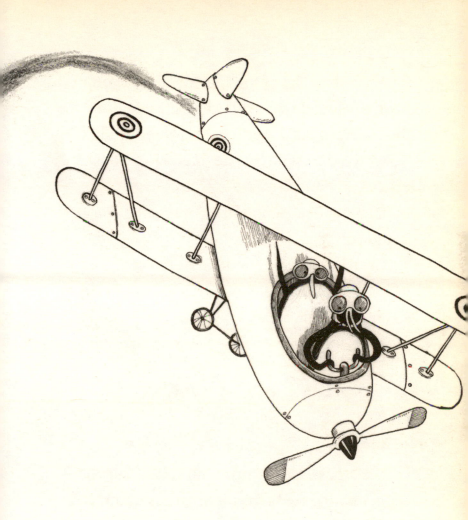

'Land on the snow, Peter. It's soft.'

'Snow is bumpy, Punky. We'll have to land on the ice!'

Peter steers the plane towards the Penguin Skating Rink. Just as the wheels hit the ice, the ice breaks and we're in the water. I think we're going to sink, but the plane just bobs about.

'Don't worry, penguins!' Peter yells. 'We're not hurt!'

The penguins are waddling about on what's left of the ice, looking at the hole and scratching their beaks.

'Peter, we've broken the Penguin Skating Rink.'

'There's still enough ice for skating, Punky.'

But then the cracks start.

The cracks spread right out to the snowy edge, and the ice breaks into pieces and the penguins drop into the water.

Peter takes off his flying goggles.

I want to be like Peter, so I take mine off too.

We jump into the icy blue water and swim across to the snowy edge, where Harold waits with his flippers folded, his eyes narrow, ready to tell Peter off. We waddle out of the water and waddle about.

'I've made the penguins a swimming pool, Harry. The plane can be repaired. We just have to lift it out of the water.'

But Harold is in a huff.

'Peter,' I say, poking Peter with my flipper, 'do you remember when we went on an explore?'

'We've been on lots of explores, Punky.'

'We went to the Jungle, did an explore, and came back.'

Peter nods his beak.

'We went in the biplane, Peter.'

'Don't talk to me about biplanes.'

'We took off over there,' I say, pointing with my flipper, 'and we flew across the snow, and across the sea to the Jungle.'

'Yes,' Peter says. 'I remember.'

'When we flew across the snow, we looked down and there was another skating rink. Do you remember?'

Peter smiles a beaky penguin smile. 'Harold! I have an idea!'

Peter tells Harold his idea, and we all waddle off across the snow, twenty penguins all in a row. It's a long way, hundreds and hundreds of waddles, and I do a belly slide, and Harold eats a fish.

But when we reach the new skating rink, it's being skated on by squiggles.

'This is the Squirrel Skating Rink,' one of the squiggles says. 'Waddle off!'

'But we want to ice skate,' Peter says.

'You wouldn't let us skate on the Penguin Skating Rink,' the squiggle says in a silly, speeded-up voice. 'Why should we let you skate on the Squirrel Skating Rink?'

Peter shrugs his flippers, and the squiggle

scampers away.

'Right,' Peter says. 'We need a plan.'

The penguins put their beaks together, and I waddle off to ice skate with the squiggles.

'Hello,' I say to one of the squiggles. 'I'm Punky. What's your name?'

'Malcolm,' the squiggle says, twitching his nose and wriggling his tail. 'What do you want?'

'Can I skate on your skating rink? Our skating rink is broken.'

'But you're not a squirrel.'

'No,' I say. 'I'm a penguin.'

Malcolm smiles a hairy squiggle smile. 'If you teach me to belly slide, you can skate on our skating rink.'

I nod my beak.

Malcolm holds out his claw, and I shake it with my flipper.

'Can my friends skate on it too?'

'Wait here,' Malcolm says. 'I will ask the other squirrels.' And off he scampers.

I slide on my belly. Then, I eat a fish. Then, Malcolm scampers back.

'The squirrels said yes,' Malcolm says. 'But be careful, the ice is thin.'

I waddle off to tell Peter, but then something bad happens. Peter waddles up to the skating rink with the other penguins waddling behind, waving their flippers and shouting. They all leap into the air and land on the ice on their bellies.

I yell at them to stop, but too late. The ice cracks and breaks, and nineteen penguins and nineteen squiggles drop into the water.

Malcolm looks at me, and I look at Malcolm.

'Squirrels can't swim,' Malcolm says in a silly, speeded-up voice.

I dive into the water. It's icy and blue,

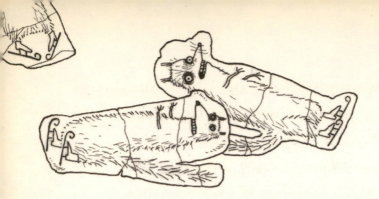

and the penguins are swimming and
the squiggles are sinking. I dive deep
and grab a squiggle's tail with my
beak and swim back up and drag
the squiggle on to the snowy edge.
Harold dives down for another
squiggle, and the other penguins do
the same until all nineteen squiggles
are rescued.

A moment later, the squiggles
have frozen solid.

'We have to thaw them out,' Harold says.

Penguin breath is warm and cosy.
We breathe toasty breath on to one
of the squiggles, and the ice melts and
the squiggle sits up. Then we do the
next squiggle and the next, until all
nineteen squiggles are scampering about
and waving their fluffy tails.

I waddle up to Peter. 'You didn't have to
do that. I asked the squiggles if we could
skate with them and they
said yes.'

Harold narrows
his eyes. 'Peter, I
was wrong about
you. You're not a
fraud. You're a fool.'

Peter looks up at the sky, at the falling
snowflakes. Then, he looks down at his feet.

'You've broken two skating rinks,' Harold
says. 'The squiggles almost drowned.'

Peter takes off the official impostor test jacket and drops it on to the snow. Then, he waddles off.

'Peter's not a fool,' I tell Harold. 'He's a pioneer.' And I waddle after Peter.

As we waddle across the snow, Peter doesn't say anything, he just looks up at the falling snowflakes, but then he fixes his eyes on me and says, 'Punky, how can you still believe in me after I ruined everything?'

I shrug my flippers.

'Well?'

'Um,' I say, waddling about. 'Because you're a pioneer.'

Peter stops mid-waddle. 'Punky, you're right. I *am* a pioneer. And I will prove it.'

We waddle back to Harold and the other penguins and Malcolm and the squiggles. Harold is breathing toasty breath on to the jacket, to dry it out.

'Harry,' Peter says, 'I will find a new

skating rink, big enough and icy
enough for twenty slidy penguins
and twenty itchy squiggles.'

Harold waddles about a bit,
breathes some more breath on to
the jacket, picks it up and gives it
to Peter.

'But that's your jacket, Harry.'

'Peter, I want you to have it.
You make a lot of mistakes, but
you have that pioneering
spirit. The jacket is yours. Now
waddle off and find us
somewhere to skate.'

Peter looks up at the
sky, at the falling
snowflakes, then fixes
his eyes on Harold
and smiles a beaky
penguin smile.

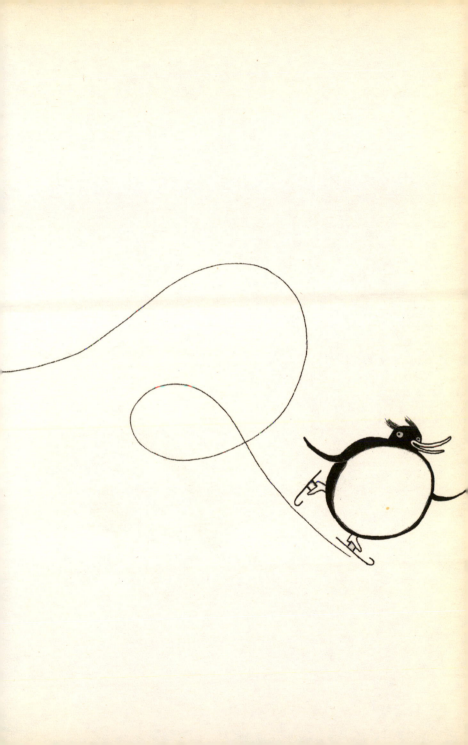